Acknowledgements:

The author wishes to thank Joan Wieszczyk, editor of The Spirit of Medjugorje,
Sister Emmanuel, and Denis Nolan, of Children of Medjugorje,
for help in trying to trace the story's origins,
and Msgr. Joseph Murray for supplying more than the words, "Per Panem Solum."

The illustrator wishes to acknowledge Csilla Sándor, editor of Csodaceruza, for
her companionable support, and she thanks Ali and her family for their loving patience.

Gingerbread House
602 Montauk Highway
Westhampton Beach, New York 11978 USA
SAN: 217-0760

Visit us at www.GingerbreadBooks.com

Art Direction and Design by Maria Nicotra and Josephine Nobisso

The illustrations were created in watercolor; the cover in mixed media.

Manufactured by Regent Publishing Services Ltd.
Printed in China

FIRST EDITION
10 9 8

Library of Congress Cataloging-in-Publication Data

Nobisso, Josephine.
   The weight of a Mass : a tale of faith / Josephine Nobisso ;
illustrated by Katalin Szegedi.
        p. cm.
Summary: On the day of a royal wedding in a kingdom where everyone has
grown careless in the practice of their Catholic faith, a poor widow
helps reveal the true value of the Mass.
   ISBN 0-940112-09-4 -- ISBN 0-940112-10-8 (pbk.)
   [1. Mass--Fiction. 2. Catholics--Fiction. 3. Faith--Fiction. 4.
Christian life--Fiction. 5. Kings, queens, rulers, etc.--Fiction.]   I.
Szegedi, Katalin, 1963- , ill. II. Title.
   PZ7.N6645 We 2002
   [Fic]--dc21
                                                        2001004925

Josephine Nobisso

THE WEIGHT OF A MASS

A Tale of Faith

Illustrated by
Katalin Szegedi

Gingerbread House
Westhampton Beach, New York

Once upon a time, a king betrothed to a queen
from a faraway land consented to be married in
the cathedral even though he knew that only
a handful of old women would attend the Holy
Mass. It was not that his subjects wished the royal
couple ill, or that they would not find their own
ways of celebrating the union, but the king's
people had grown cold and careless in the practice
of their faith.

A while before the ceremony, a ragged old widow shuffled into the kingdom's most prosperous bakeshop. Subjects soaring in high spirits and decked in finery whisked past her, carrying away the finest confections and loaves of bread.

The baker lifted elegant pastries, and arranged them in lacy boxes upon which he tied jaunty bows. His son, a kindly boy, guarded the royal wedding cake from children's probing fingers, all the while describing how he and his father had erected it.

Finally, it was the widow's turn in the crowded shop. "For the love of God," she begged of the baker, "if you will give me a crust of stale bread, I will offer my Mass tonight for you."

The baker's son spun on his heels to fetch the bread reserved for children who fed the royal swans, but his father growled, "This woman shares the disease from which you suffer and your mother before you! If I didn't keep you busy here, I'd find you on your knees in church, with the likes of her!"

A hush fell over the crowd. The baker peered over the counter. "You propose to hear a Mass for me?" he challenged the old woman.

"I'd rather hear the jingle of your coins!"

"But I haven't a schilling!" the widow whispered.

"Then I haven't the bread!" the baker shot back.

"Father!" the son protested, "She asked in the name of God!"

"Then let God provide her bread!" the baker exclaimed.

The widow turned to leave, but the baker had not finished taunting her. "Let us see how much bread I would owe you!" he said. He tore a tiny corner off his finest tissue paper, and read aloud as he formed two miniscule words: "One Mass."

The baker held up the tiny piece of paper, and with a ceremonious flair, he laid the wispy scrap onto the resting tray of his brass scale. He then flicked a slice of old bread onto the other tray. He blinked, confused. The bread side had not dropped to lift the lighter paper.

"Impossible!" the baker exclaimed, placing a marzipan apple onto the bread's side. Still, the tray holding the paper stayed down. The baker piled layered cake onto the tray, but this did not tip the scale.

He stacked his best cherry-topped cupcakes onto the balance, but they did not make the difference.

Brushing past his son, he swept heavy, filled chocolates into a box. Still, the scale did not budge when he placed those on it, too. He arranged a dozen poppy seed cakes and two-dozen rolls onto the pile.
"The paper outweighs his goods!" a man exclaimed.

"The Royal Council of Weights and Measures tested this scale just last week!" the baker protested. "Something's gone wrong with it!"

The baker's son lifted the tiny scrap of paper off the scale, and a gasp went up as the baked goods crashed down with a jangle. Everyone began speaking at once. "What can this mean?" they asked each other.

The crowd quieted to watch as the baker emptied the heavy tray and tested the scale with all his weights, even those

smaller than game pieces. The scale
responded to every change, floating up
and down. "The scale is correct!"
a woman exclaimed.
"Of course it's correct!"
the baker bellowed.
"I'm an honest man!"

Compelled by the event, clients rushed to the doors, calling in more witnesses from the streets.

The baker addressed his son, "Pile it high! This time turn the scale around so that the trays are switched!" The breads and buns, candies, and cakes brought their side down with a satisfying thud.

"Now," the baker said as he let the snippet of paper float down toward the new tray, "We'll see the truth!"

No sooner did the tissue touch the shiny brass tray than it lifted the opposite one. "But I don't understand!" the baker muttered as he ran to fetch his freshest donuts. He piled on fruitcakes and cream cakes, berry tarts and poached pears. "This can't be!" he cried as he plastered on plum pudding and candied fruits, almond confetti and crushed walnuts.

"The Mass intention weighs more than these!" the baker's son marveled.

The baker was beside himself with bewilderment. He turned to his son. "Don't think I don't know that you would abandon the baking trade to become a priest!" he warned. "And don't think any of this will influence me!" He took a deep breath. "Bring me the royal wedding cake!"

As the baker's son rolled the cake's cart through the crowd, it parted, respectful lest the prized confection get damaged.

"On the count of three," the baker ordered his son, "help me get it onto the scale. This will put an end to the nonsense!"

"One! Two! Three!"

The wedding cake teetered on the top of the pile. The paper on which the baker had written the words, "One Mass" hadn't even fluttered. The baker and his clients stood, dumb-founded.

Just then, the cathedral bell began tolling the call to the royal wedding Mass. The baker's son stood over the piece of paper, staring at it. When he lifted it from the scale, hands surged forward to rescue the wedding cake as the things beneath it crashed down with a weighty clang. A man went out into the street and took up the *Ave Maria* the bells were tolling. Other clients, who had intended to celebrate the royal wedding in diverse ways, now filed out and processed toward the kingdom's great cathedral. One

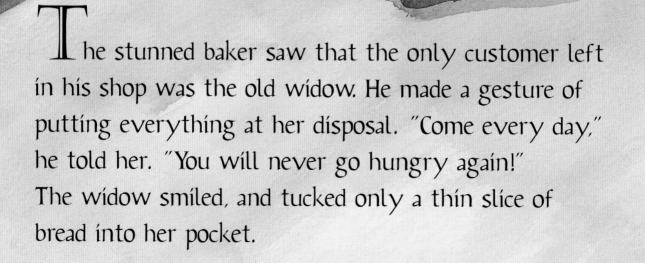

The stunned baker saw that the only customer left
in his shop was the old widow. He made a gesture of
putting everything at her disposal. "Come every day,"
he told her. "You will never go hungry again!"
The widow smiled, and tucked only a thin slice of
bread into her pocket.

As the baker watched his son unbutton his white apron, the father sensed that—one day—the boy would be exchanging it for a white collar.

The baker, his son, and the widow trailed the procession to the cathedral, to offer Mass with their monarchs. Amidst the singing and the exclamations of wonder and joy, the baker asked the old lady, "Why did you take only a slice when you could have had anything and everything in my shop?"

"I was ashamed to take more," the widow told him.

"Ashamed?" the baker asked. "But it was you who believed in God's power while the rest of us had grown cold!"

"I was ashamed," the widow explained, "because even though I have never given up going to Mass, I asked you only for a crust of stale bread in exchange for it.

"You see, my friend—like you—I, too, do not know the weight of a Mass."

Author's Postscript

Every culture has "its" stories—fairy tales, fables and parables—that speak of the larger issues and ideas of a people of like mind, and that give other traditions a glimpse into those beliefs.

Children often ask me where I "got the idea" for a story. The inspiration to write the original fable, The Weight of a Mass, A Tale of Faith, came in 1998, while reading a piece in The Spirit of Medjugorje Newsletter. It recounted the story of a certain Father Stanislaus, SS. CC. In his town in Luxembourg, a conversation between the butcher and a Captain of the Forest Guards was interrupted when an old woman entered the butcher shop to beg a morsel of meat. When the butcher scoffed at the poor woman, she offered to hear Holy Mass in exchange for the meat. The events that transpired then were very similar to what happens in our own story here, which I have set, instead, in a bakery, on the day when a king is to marry a queen from a devout kingdom.

As a result of the butcher shop miracle, the Captain began attending Mass daily, and one of his sons later received a calling to the priesthood. That captain had been Father Stanislaus' own father.

The Holy Sacrifice of the Mass—The Eucharistic Celebration—is the priceless, "source and summit of the Christian life" because in it, Christ Himself is truly present. In its unfathomably deep richness lies the perfect fulfillment of Jesus' command to repeat His actions and words until He comes.[†]

Sia lodato Gesù Cristo!   [†]Catechism of the Catholic Church 1324-1341

Dedications
For Our Lady, and for all her consecrated
sons, especially those from whom,
in recent years, my family has had
the blessing of growth in the Faith. -JN

For my Grandma,
who knew the weight of a Mass. -KSz